To Tonia, who saved my life

Atheneum Books for Young Readers
An imprint of Simon & Schuster Children's
Publishing Division
1230 Avenue of the Americas
New York, New York 10020

Copyright © 2006 by Ian Falconer
"Simple Plan" used with permission of Simple
Plan and Lava Records, LLC. This image is
a composite of three photographs, each used
with permission of the copyright owners:
© Lava Records (photo by Patrick Langlois),
© 2006 Robert E. Klein, and © Steve Russell.
Bowling Green High School Bobcat Marching
Band © 2003 by Michael D. Coomes.
"Silver and Blue Skyworks" © Katrina Leigh;
"Fireworks" © Joe Stone; "Red, White, Blue
Fireworks" © Gary Brown; and "Fireworks 3"
© Brian Prawl. Portrait of US Supreme Court
Justices © 2006 Diana Walker/Time & Life
Pictures/Getty Images

Book design by Ann Bobco
The text of this book is set in Centaur.
The illustrations of this book are rendered in
charcoal and gouache on paper.

Manufactured in the United States of America
First Edition
10 9 8 7 6 5 4 3 2 1
CIP date for this book is available from the
Library of Congress.
ISBN-13: 978-1-4169-2454-8
ISBN-10: 1-4169-2454-X

OLIVIA
forms a band

by Ian Falconer

An Anne Schwartz Book
Atheneum Books for Young Readers
New York   London   Toronto   Sydney

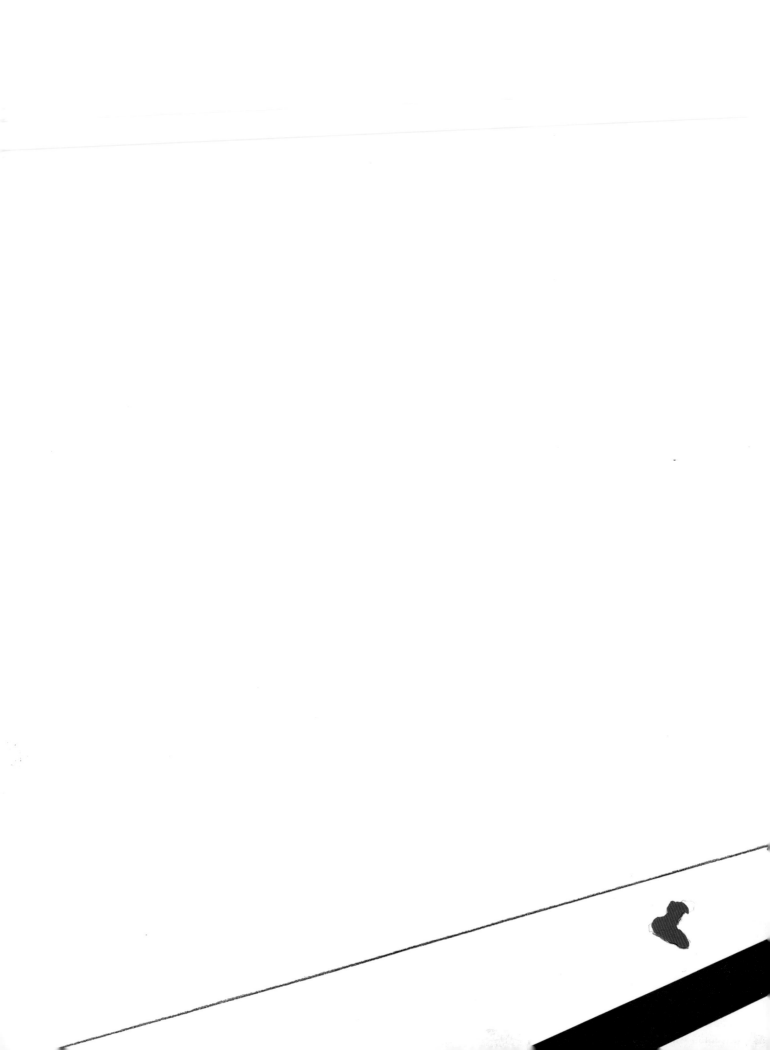

Olivia couldn't find her other red sock.

"What's the matter?" asked her mother.
"I can't find my other red sock," said Olivia.
"What are those all over the floor?"
"They don't go with this one."

"I found it!"

Olivia's mother was packing a picnic.
"I want everyone ready by seven
for the fireworks," she said.
"And the band!" cried Olivia.

"Oh, I don't think there will
be a band," said her mother.

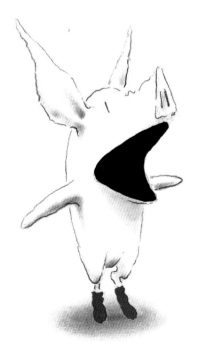

"But you can't have fireworks
without a band," explained Olivia.

"I know!
We'll be the band!"

"Fine," said Olivia. "I'll be the band."

"What kind of band
are you thinking of?"
asked her mother.

"A fireworks band,
of course."

"But, sweetheart, one person can't be a whole band," said Olivia's mother.
"Why not?"
"Because the word 'band' means more than one person, and a band *sounds* like more than one person."

"This morning you told me I sounded like five people!"

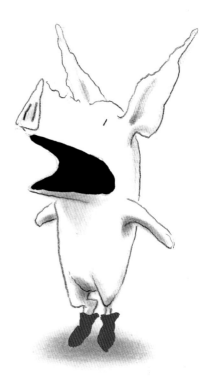

All day long Olivia gathered everything she needed to make her band.

"Thank you."

"Thank you."

"Look, Daddy,
we're twins."

Finally she was finished.
All that was left was to choose the perfect outfit.

And when she marched in, everyone agreed that
Olivia *did* sound like more than one person.

To Olivia, she sounded just like a real band.

Tempo marziale.

At seven o'clock Olivia's mother was trying to get everyone into the car. "Olivia, aren't you going to bring your band?" she asked.

"I don't feel like it."

"Well, don't forget to put everything away,"
her mother said.
"Okay, Mommy."
"Where are you going?"
"I have to put on my make-up," said Olivia.
"All right, sweetheart, but hurry."

The final touch ...

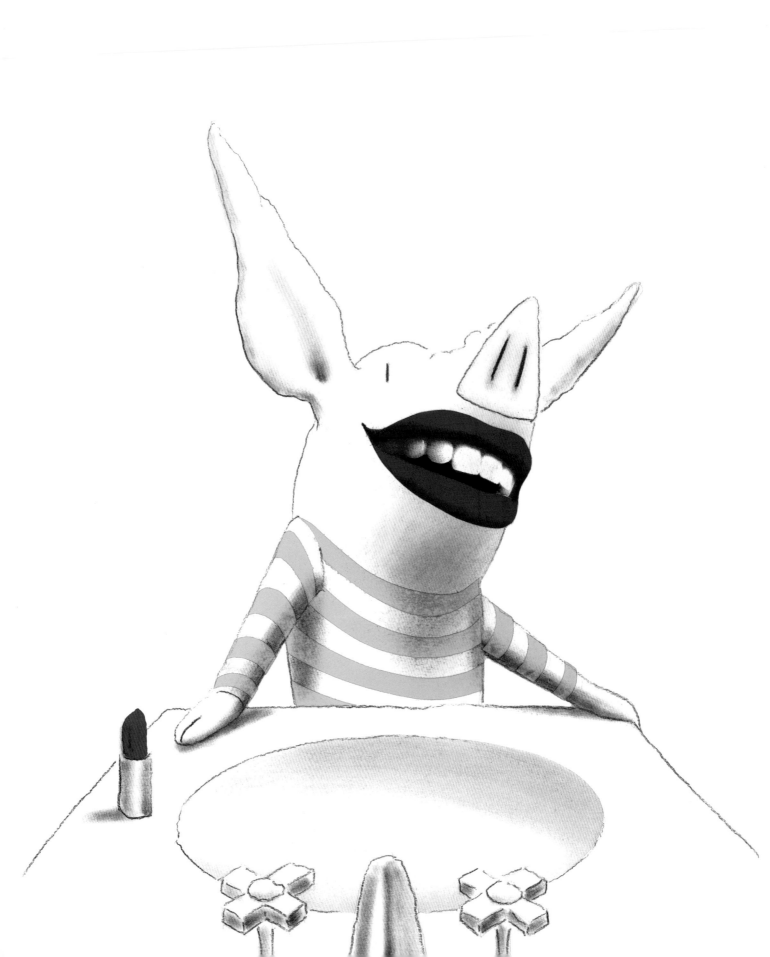

Of course, when they got there . . .

Olivia said,
"Mommy,
I have to go
to the
bathroom."

And, of course,
then Ian said
he had
to go to the
bathroom too.

William just went to the bathroom.

The sun was setting. They ate sandwiches and corn on the cob and strawberries and watermelon.

"When are the fireworks going to start?" asked Olivia.
"When it gets dark," explained her mother.
"When will it be dark?"
"Soon, sweetheart."
"Is it dark yet?"
"Almost. Be patient."

"*Now* is it dark?"

Finally
the fireworks started.

And they were beautiful.

It was very late when everyone got home.

"Go climb into bed, sweetheart," said Olivia's mother.
"No books tonight."

"Aren't you going
to come kiss me
good night?"
asked Olivia.

"In a minute—and don't forget to put your band away."

After Ian and William were tucked into bed, Olivia's mother tiptoed into Olivia's room . . .

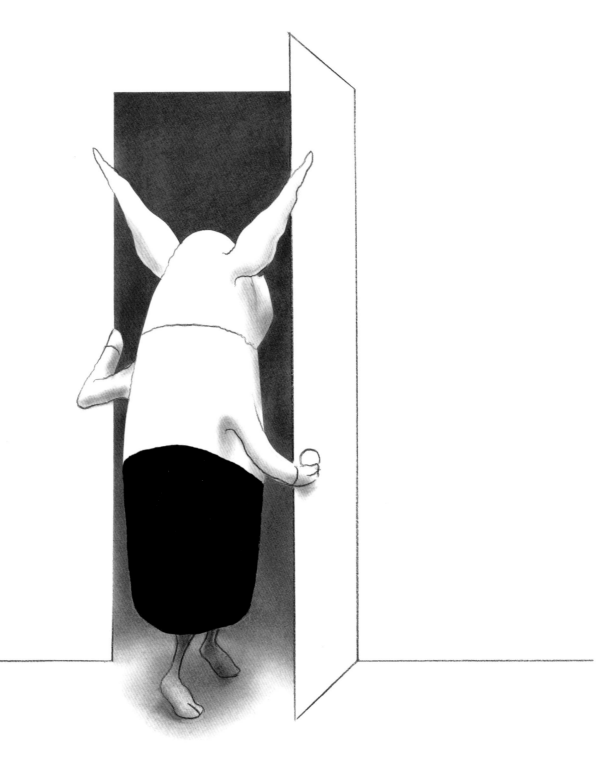

"OLIVIA, I told you to put your band away.
I could have broken my neck!"

But Olivia was fast asleep.

The End